Kathryn the Grape's Piece of Love

Story created and written by Kathryn Cloward
Illustrated by Christine Winscott

kandonpublishing

For Landon.
You inspired me to write this story.
You are my greatest inspiration.
I love you.
·KC·

To Shonah and Meghan
(with Brian and Dave).
Thank you for the joy of
Connor, Isabella, Ewan, Anwen and Esu.
You are all the sprinkles
on my cupcake of life!
·CW·

A special note
of gratitude
to Jennie Lapointe for
her creative contribution
to this book, and to
Cindy MacDonald
and Jennifer Harris
for their editing
assistance.

www.KathryntheGrape.com

Kathryn the Grape

Kathryn the Grape's Piece of Love
is published by Kandon Publishing,
a division of Kandon Unlimited, Inc.

Copyright © 2012 by Kandon Unlimited, Inc.

Library of Congress Control Number: 2012912538

ISBN-13: 978-0-9829277-2-4
ISBN-10: 098292772X
Printed in China 8-2012

Cover art
and
book layout
by
Christine Winscott

The
characters
in this book
are based on
real people.

Hi!
I'm Kathryn the Grape.
Purple is my favorite color and I wear it every day.
This is my best friend, Maggie.
She is a magical butterfly.

Maggie gave me a magic wand and a magical charm bracelet
to help me discover how magical and *colorful* I am.

3

"Come on. Let's go," Keshi yelled
when the recess bell finished ringing.
Landon and I slid down the slide
one last time and ran
to catch up with Keshi.

4

"That was fun! Let's play pirates again during lunch," Landon suggested.
As we got in line with our class I said,
"It was fun! But we've been pirates for two days. Let's play circus instead, ok?"

Keshi nodded her head with excitement. She stretched her arms out wide as she slowly walked away imagining, "I will be the tightrope walker."

Landon wanted to be the ringmaster.

He cleared his throat and with a deep voice said,

"Ladies and gentlemen, boys and girls, welcome to Circus Encanto."

I knew exactly who I wanted to be!
"I will be the motorcycle rider,
the one in the cage
that goes around and around
in circles really fast."

We were all excited and agreed
that lunch time would be circus time for our Adventure Club!

When we got back to our classroom, Mrs. Vega told us that our creative writing lesson would be the final piece of the "Our Planet, Our Home" series.

All month long we had been studying planet Earth and learning how everything is connected. We are all responsible, she taught us, for doing our part in caring for our planet, and for each other.

Mrs. Vega explained that we were each going to receive a large puzzle piece. One side of the puzzle piece had part of the puzzle's picture. The other side had a blank space for us to write an answer to the question written on the board.

When we were done, we would share our answers with the rest of the class. Then, as a group, we would put the puzzle together to see the big picture.

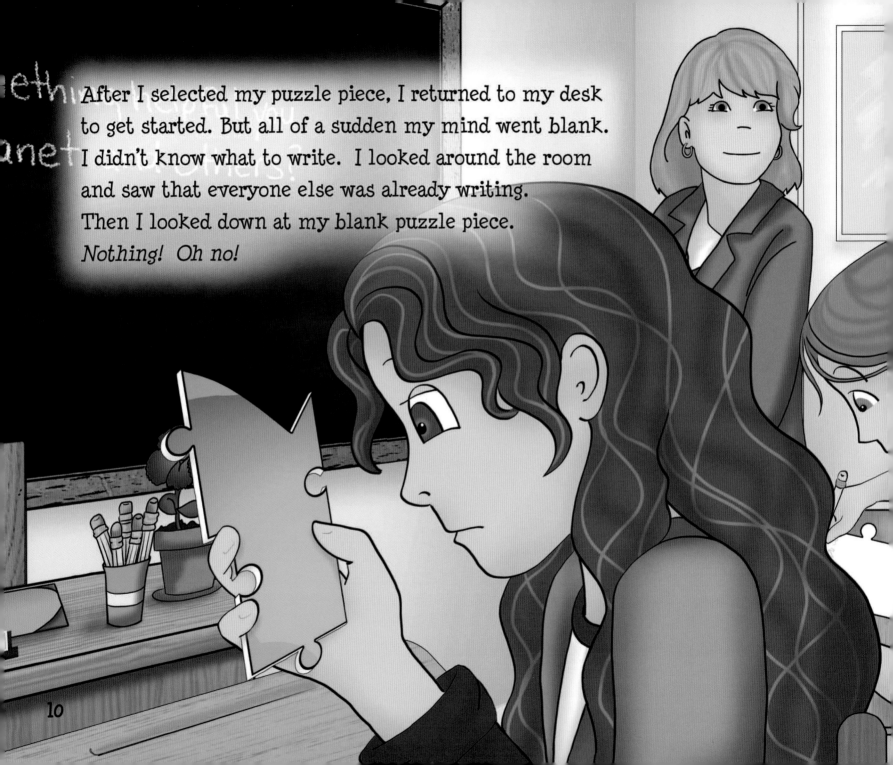

After I selected my puzzle piece, I returned to my desk to get started. But all of a sudden my mind went blank. I didn't know what to write. I looked around the room and saw that everyone else was already writing. Then I looked down at my blank puzzle piece. *Nothing! Oh no!*

10

"What's bothering you, Kathryn the Grape?" Maggie asked.

"I want to write something really good, but I can't think of anything. What am I going to do? What if I don't finish the assignment?" Big nervous bubbles moved around in my stomach as I imagined standing in front of my class with nothing to share while my classmates laughed at me.

Maggie put her hand on mine and said,
"You are thinking too much and letting
worry sneak into your thoughts.
Trust yourself
and allow words to flow...
let your sun charm shine.
Do you remember what
I told you happens
when you worry?"
"I know. I know," I sighed.

"But we all need to be reminded of things sometimes," Maggie explained. "When you worry, you *think* about negative outcomes to a situation. Worry blocks what is naturally designed to flow. Right now, your worried thoughts are interrupting your creative energy."

She continued, "When a beaver builds a dam in a river, the dam blocks the natural flow of the river's water. You are a beaver, my dear. You are building a dam of worry instead of letting your river of creativity flow. Does that make sense?"

13

I thought about what Maggie was saying, and I remembered seeing a beaver dam last summer while on my family camping trip. One afternoon we floated down the nearby river on tubes. My brothers and I sang songs and played games as we drifted down the river. It was so much fun!

14

But at one point, the river was blocked and it was too narrow
for us to float any longer. We had to get off of our tubes
to walk around all of the branches and rocks that were in our way.
Maggie was right! Beaver dams do block a river's natural flow.

I looked at Maggie and said, "It does make sense. But what am I supposed to do? If my worried thoughts are blocking my creative writing, how am I supposed to get rid of them?"

Maggie nodded. "That's a great question, Kathryn the Grape. To get unstuck, you simply have to tell the beavers to go away. And remind them to take their branches with them."

I laughed. "What? What are you talking about, Maggie?"

"Look! There they are," Maggie exclaimed pointing to my blank puzzle piece.

I could barely believe what I was seeing! There were beavers on my puzzle piece! I looked at Maggie with amazement. Then I looked at the beavers and politely said to them, "Hello, beavers. I have work I need to do, and you are in my way. It is time for you to leave. Please be sure to take all of your branches with you. Goodbye!"

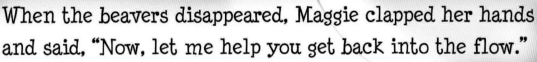

When the beavers disappeared, Maggie clapped her hands and said, "Now, let me help you get back into the flow."

Guiding me, she told me to put both of my feet on the floor, close my eyes, and take ten deep breaths.
"Breathe in slowly and imagine your belly blowing up like a balloon. Then breathe out slowly as if you are deflating your belly balloon."

When I was all ready to start, Maggie had one last instruction. "While you are doing that, try to clear your mind of every thought, Kathryn the Grape."

Every thought, I wondered.
Wow! That was going to be difficult.
But Maggie has never steered me wrong before, so I tried to do what she suggested.

I slowly took my first deep breath in, then let it out.

I did it again....and again...and again.

I did it ten times.

Then I opened my eyes. I felt calm and refreshed.
I picked up my pen, looked down at my puzzle piece, and knew
exactly what I wanted to write. I was back in the flow.

When it was time to share, Keshi raised her hand
to go first. "My piece is acceptance.
My parents taught me never to think
that I am better than or less than anyone else.
I believe that everyone should be treated equally."
Keshi continued sharing about her family
and about how her parents adopted her
from China and her brother from Ethiopia.

I felt so happy that she was my friend
because Keshi is truly accepting of everyone.
One by one everyone else shared their puzzle pieces.

Cael does his chores without being asked.

Talia and her little brother recycle at home.

Leila Joy donates her clothes to the shelter downtown.

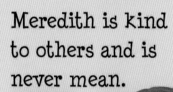

Meredith is kind to others and is never mean.

Kai gives his toys to children who don't have any.

Isha saves energy at home by turning off unused lights.

21

Paxton doesn't use plastic bags.

Alyssa volunteers at her church.

Toni picks up trash whenever she sees it on the ground.

Esu plants trees with his scouting troop at the community park.

Landon helps his friends when they are in need.

Ben takes shorter showers and doesn't waste water.

Sana no longer drinks out of plastic water bottles.

Jordan helps her grandma in their vegetable garden.

Tara volunteers at the community shelter with her moms.

Samantha is a vegetarian and likes to protect animals.

Then it was my turn. I stood in front of my class and felt a few nervous bubbles again. I quickly used my magic wand to make them go away as I began to read the words I wrote on my puzzle piece.

What is something helpful you do for our planet and others?

Home

ts

oday

eports

project

24

My friend Maggie
told me how important
it is to be loving and
kind to others.
She taught me that just like
a rock dropped into water creates
ripples, every day I am creating
ripples too. I now understand that
my thoughts, words, and actions
have a ripple effect, and it is up to me to choose
what my ripple effect is. When I think positive thoughts, say
nice words, and do kind things, I am
rippling loving kindness into the world.
This is how I help others and the planet.

This is my piece of love.

25

As I sat down at my desk, Maggie fluttered over. "I am proud of you, Kathryn the Grape. You overcame the blocking beavers, got into the flow, and shared beautiful words with your classmates. Did you know that it is not just your heart that is full of love? You are full of love because **you are love.** In fact, *everyone* is love! That is why it's easy to ripple loving kindness."

I smiled and believed it to be true.

My friend Maggie told me how important it is to be loving and kind to others. She taught me that just like a rock dropped into water creates ripples, every day I am creating ripples too. I now understand that my thoughts, words, and actions have a ripple effect, and it is up to me to choose what my ripple effect is. When I think positive thoughts, say nice words, and do kind things into the world. This is how I help others and the planet.

This is my piece of love.

I am **MAGICAL**.
I am **COLORFUL**.
I am **LOVE**.
I am
Kathryn the Grape.

27

When Mrs. Vega invited us to gather around to connect our puzzle pieces, Maggie whispered, "Imagine what it would be like if everyone chose to ripple loving kindness every day."

We all gathered around
to help put the puzzle together.
All of our pieces connected perfectly.
Maggie handed me a silver coin and said, "This
magical coin is for you, Kathryn the Grape.
Always have it with you as a reminder that you are love."
"Thank you, Maggie! I will carry it in my
pocket every day. But how is this coin magical?" I wondered.
Smiling she whispered, "The coin is magical because magical
things happen when you ripple loving kindness into the world."

Soon, the bell rang for lunch.
As we grabbed our lunch sacks, Landon asked,
"Are we still going to play circus?"
Keshi looked at me and we both nodded and smiled.

"Good," Landon exclaimed as Keshi skipped off behind him.
Before I left our classroom, I looked back at our puzzle hanging on the wall
and could see the big picture clearly.

We are love.